T0354440

The Invisible
Trap

Written by **John Clay**

Illustrated by **Milan Samadder**

 MOONEYEDESIGNHOUSE.COM

Archway Publishing books may be ordered through booksellers or by contacting:

Archway Publishing
1663 Liberty Drive
Bloomington, IN 47403
www.archwaypublishing.com
844-669-3957

Because of the dynamic nature of the Internet, any web addresses or links contained in this book may have changed since publication and may no longer be valid. The views expressed in this work are solely those of the author and do not necessarily reflect the views of the publisher, and the publisher hereby disclaims any responsibility for them.

Any people depicted in stock imagery provided by Getty Images are models, and such images are being used for illustrative purposes only.
Certain stock imagery © Getty Images.

Interior Image Credit: Milan Samadder

ISBN: 978-1-6657-3535-3 (sc)
ISBN: 978-1-6657-3536-0 (hc)
ISBN: 978-1-6657-3537-7 (e)

Print information available on the last page.

Archway Publishing rev. date: 12/28/2022

Yelling and singing, there once was a boy.
Energy overflowing, he was so full of joy.

Pillaging and plundering all through the house,
he drove his mom crazy, just like a mouse.

2

She opened the door and pushed him outside.
He shot like a cannon, taking great strides.

3

Across the backyard and over a stream,
he ran and he sprinted with a full head of steam.

He saw a tall tree and started to climb it,
but it was too tall; and he began to feel frightened.

"I can't climb this tree, I'm not brave or real strong!
I'll go back down, which is where I belong."

One second, he was climbing the next he was not.
He looked at his laces, they were tied in a knot.

He tried to undo them, but the knot was too tangled.
He couldn't undo it, he tried from all angles.

Soon he grew angry, frustrated, and scared.
His mom would be calling, and he wouldn't be there.

Would she remember that he had gone out?
Where would she look for him, around and about?

9

Alone in the dark, what could he do?
He looked all around, from his tall view.
No matter his effort, he couldn't get free.
Soon a voice spoke. Did it come from the tree?

Sometimes you'll be lonely, and sometimes you'll be scared,
but I will protect you, no matter how unprepared.
Just take a quick moment to rest and find peace,
the answer is often hidden, which means...

The knot is just something that hides the truth.
The answer to the question may already be in view.

It comes from a voice we often don't hear.
It provides peace and joy, which conquers all fear.

When you are frantic, anxious, and blue,
there are words that offer comfort; and a message which is true.

The MOST BIGGEST problems can't be found on a map.
They're dangers well hidden; they're INVISIBLE TRAPS!

The knot is just a symbol of another real threat.
This danger is the belief that forms in your head.
Beliefs can be hard to understand and unravel,
They can be traps and leave you feeling rattled.

They make us feel scared, not letting us see.
They're the real reason, not letting us be,

the boy in the house, just like the mouse,
who drove his mom crazy, before he went out.

Thanks to the Voice, the INVISIBLE TRAP could be seen,
It was the belief he embraced which was absurd and obscene,
He knew was strong, brave, and more too!
He can handle this little knot and look at this view!

One moment he was anxious; the next, he was free.
The laces were not stuck, just caught on a tree.

With a little less struggle and no more despair,
he could see the solution to the tiny little snare.

With a tug, a twist, and a quick little yank,
his freedom was given, and the Voice he did thank.

He looked all around, but no one was there.
He thought for a moment but could only stare.

It was obvious, quite simple; he knew it to be true.
His Father's voice was with him, and He knew what to do.

We should trust in His Word and have faith in His plans.
Lean into his comfort without making demands.

So, if you are lonely, struggling, and scared,
remember He's with you in your moment of despair.
He sees the whole forest and knows where you are.
No matter how lost, it's never too far.

The INVISIBLE TRAP can be dangerous when unseen,
Yet the Father is an Expert, who always intervenes.

Trust you'll escape from the trap into the light,
where all is calm and beautiful and bright.

24

About the Author

John served in the US Army from 2011 until 2022. The impact of his service left him angry, frustrated, and scared. In 2017 his first daughter was born. He realized he needed to address his emotional trauma. That's when he discovered his own Invisible Trap.

Printed in the United States
by Baker & Taylor Publisher Services